The Fairy House
Fairy Friends

Welcome to the Fairy House –
a whole new magical world...

Look out for all *The Fairy House* books:

FAIRY FRIENDS
FAIRY FOR A DAY
FAIRIES TO THE RESCUE
FAIRY RIDING SCHOOL

Other books by Kelly McKain

Mermaid Rock:
PIRATE TROUBLE
SPOOKY SHIPWRECK
TREASURE HUNT
WHALE RESCUE

Make sure you visit www.thefairyhouse.co.uk
for competitions, prizes and lots more fairy fun!

The Fairy House
Fairy Friends

Kelly McKain

Illustrated by Nicola Slater

SCHOLASTIC

First published in 2007 by Scholastic Children's Books
An imprint of Scholastic Ltd
Euston House, 24 Eversholt Street, London, NW1 1DB, UK
Registered office: Westfield Road, Southam, Warwickshire, CV47 0RA
SCHOLASTIC and associated logos are trademarks and/or registered trademarks of Scholastic Inc.

Text copyright © Kelly McKain, 2007
Cover and inside illustrations copyright © Nicola Slater, 2007

The rights of Kelly McKain and Nicola Slater to be identified respectively
as the author and illustrator of this work have been asserted by them.

10 digit ISBN 0 439 94350 7
13 digit ISBN 978 0439 94350 5

British Library Cataloguing-in-Publication Data
A CIP catalogue record for this book is available from the British Library

Printed and bound by Imago
Papers used by Scholastic Children's Books are made
from wood grown in sustainable forests.

1 3 5 7 9 10 8 6 4 2

www.scholastic.co.uk/zone

For

Jill, Katie and Lew the Chew, with love

With thanks to

Amanda Punter, Katy Moran, Elaine McQuade, Andrew Biscomb, Georgia Lawe, Sarah Spedding, Kate Wilson, Claire Tagg, Eleanor Schramm, and Hilary Murray-Hill for working your magic on this, and for loving Fairy House as much as I do! xx

Chapter 1

Katie twisted the ring Auntie Jane had given her round and round on her finger, as she always did when she was nervous. The parcel just *had* to come today.

At last she heard the postman crunching along the neat gravel driveway, but she was far too shy to go running up to him. Instead she listened to Mum answering the door, and the postman asking how they were settling in. They'd

only been in the new house two weeks.

The new house really was a *new* house – just built. Katie found it strange that no one had ever used the cooker or the bath before they got there. The house looked exactly the same as all the others on the small estate, except that Mum had painted the front door a vibrant pink. In the fairy tales Katie loved reading, the houses always had secret passageways or hidden cupboards to explore, but in their own, every single nook and cranny was crammed with their things.

As soon as she heard the front door closing, Katie hurried into the hall. She didn't have to ask if the parcel had come – Mum was clutching a large brown-paper-

wrapped box! Katie knew it was what she'd been waiting for. A new house of her very own.

The moment Mum put the box down Katie pounced on it and tore off the paper. She could feel her heart pounding as she wrenched the box open, reached inside and pulled. Then there it was, the dolls' house!

It was made of pink plastic with little cut-out windows and it had a yellow door with a tiny blue handle. Katie pressed down a catch on the roof and the whole front of the house swung open. Inside was a kitchen and living room, and stairs to the bedrooms above. "Four bedrooms! Just like our house," she cried, then added, "I mean, our old house."

"There's more inside the box," said Mum.

Katie delved in again and rummaged around. She fished out packet after packet of tiny furniture – a sofa, beds, a table, wardrobes, kitchen cupboards, a grand piano.

Katie traced her hand over the pink tiled plastic roof – it was finally here, her very own dolls' house! She'd been thinking and even dreaming about one for absolutely ages – and asking and asking and asking, of course! Even though it wasn't anywhere near her birthday, Mum had finally given in and said she could have one for being so helpful with the move.

Together they set

out all the dolls'-house furniture on the table. "There's everything you need to make a lovely home right here," said Mum.

"Yes, it's great, it's just a bit plain, that's all," Katie murmured. She thought for a moment, then had an idea. "Oh, I know!" she cried. "I can make it more unusual, so there's only one like it in the whole world. I'll paint the door, and make curtains, and do pictures to go on the walls, just like you did with this place!"

Mum was an artist, so she really had created the vividly coloured canvases that hung on their walls.

"Great idea," said Mum. "Look, it's a lovely day, why don't you take everything outside and get some fresh air?"

So Katie ran upstairs and grabbed

her paints and brushes and stickers and glitter and glue. She scooped up a handful of Barbies too, then realized they'd be far too big to fit into the dolls' house. She stopped still – she hadn't even thought about *dolls*. What good was a dolls' house if she had no dolls to actually live in it? Then she was struck with another great idea – she'd make some!

She picked up some bits of card from her desk (Mum always cut up the old cereal boxes for her), and her school pencil case with her blunt gluey scissors and felt pens

inside. She galloped downstairs and rummaged in the craft drawer for the bag of fabric offcuts. She could use the scraps to dress her dolls, and for making curtains, too, and maybe even bedspreads! Katie's heart was pounding again – who wanted a stuffy old dolls' house that was already perfect anyway? This would be much more fun!

Katie put all her things inside the pink plastic house, shut the latch and picked it up by the handle, like a suitcase. Then she headed outside. The garden was just a neat rectangle of turf, though Mum was planning borders and climbing plants and maybe even a vegetable patch. The developers had only put a thin strip of wire up as a back fence, and the neighbours soon changed theirs for tall wooden panels that still smelled like that funny brown paint you put on them. But Mum liked the open feel and kept the wire, which made it so easy for Katie to bob underneath.

Beyond the fence was a patch of rough ground that hadn't been built on. It wasn't really big enough to call a meadow, but the grass was high and full of poppies, dandelions and foxgloves, and at the centre stood a grand old oak tree. Katie had discovered it the day they moved in. It was the perfect place for daydreaming, playing and making things.

Since no one else ever went there, Katie was starting to think of it as her own special, private place. She swished through the grass and set the dolls' house down under the tree, then she clicked it open and pulled out her art things.

And there, with the breeze rustling the leaves above her and insects buzzing happily around, Katie spent a lovely morning making the dolls' house her very own. First she painted the front door a brilliant purple. Then she stuck silver heart and star stickers on the

plain pink furniture and arranged it in the different rooms, singing her favourite songs as she worked.

Next she started on the cardboard dolls, drawing out the shapes and then cutting carefully around them. She made four – one for each bedroom. Then she tipped her bag of fabric scraps out on to the uneven, tree-rooty ground and chose the material for their outfits. Two were getting groovy jeans and two were going to have funky skirts and tops. The cardboard dolls would have parties in the house all the time, Katie decided. She'd make them little paper hats and decorations and

even a tiny pass-the-parcel!

Planning her dolls' first party was such fun – but it made her feel lonely too. She wished she had someone to share it with, but her old friends were all back in London, busy with the end of term play. It was so unfair – she was supposed to be Cinderella, but the move to Dorset meant she was missing it all. Hannah Williams had snaffled the role instead.

Her new school wasn't *that* bad, she supposed, but she found everything there so new and strange – their rough work books were blue instead of orange, the lunch hall smelled different and you had a separate peg for your PE kit in the cloakroom. Her teacher, Mrs Borthwick, was a big cheerful lady with leggings and a grey blunt-cut bob, and most of the children seemed nice too, but she hadn't made any real friends yet. She missed having girls to whisper secrets to and make presents for and play made-up games with.

"I must find a friend before the school holidays," she told herself firmly, picturing the hot, lonely weeks stretching out in front of her.

For a moment, Katie had the strangest feeling, as if she were being watched. She glanced all around her, but no one was there. She shrugged and began cutting out a stripy skirt and singing a new song, the one about the kookaburra and the old gum tree. She didn't even get to the second verse before she heard Mum calling her in to lunch.

Mum sounded so worried that Katie instantly leapt up, shouting, "Here I am! Over the fence!" She hurried inside, meaning to come back out straight afterwards.

But once she'd eaten her fish fingers and beans and helped with the drying up they went to visit Auntie Jane. They all ended up going for a long walk then staying for tea and when they got home it was already bath time. By the time Mum had detangled and dried Katie's long brown hair, it was past bedtime and she said lights out straight away, as there was no time

for a story. Just as she was falling asleep, Katie remembered that the dolls' house was still under the oak tree. But she was too tired to get up again and fetch it in – so that's where it stayed.

First thing the next morning, Katie wanted to get straight on with her dolls' house project – there were the dolls' outfits to finish, and she hadn't even started on the curtains. She gave Mum a good morning hug and tried to hurry out of the back door – but Mum insisted she have a bowl of cereal first! Soon enough, though, Katie was outside, slipping through the wire fence and wading across the grassy meadow to the oak tree.

And that's when she got a huge surprise.

Her cardboard dolls were lying on the ground by the front door – and yet she was sure she'd left them safely inside the dolls' house, in their bedrooms.

Stranger still, there were blue polka-dot curtains hanging at a bedroom window.

Curtains she hadn't made.

Katie felt her stomach flip over. Had someone been here in the night, messing with her things? Suddenly something caught her attention. Strange sounds. Almost like *voices*. She froze, listening. But all she could hear were birds

singing in the trees and insects buzzing through the flowers.

But . . . aha! There it was again! Definitely voices, she was sure now. At first Katie thought they were coming from far away, but then she realized that they were very *close*, but just very *tiny*. They sounded beautiful – almost magical – like crystal wind chimes tinkling in the breeze.

Katie listened hard. She gasped. The voices were *right beside her*.

They were coming from *inside* the dolls' house.

Chapter 2

Katie lay down on her stomach and peered through the kitchen window. She gasped in amazement.

She blinked and stared and blinked again.

She absolutely and utterly could NOT believe her eyes.

Inside the kitchen were four tiny creatures with shimmering wings and beautiful silky petal skirts!

Fairies!

But how could they be? It just wasn't possible! Katie knew that fairies were only in books, not real life! And yet here they were, in her very own dolls' house! Could they really have thrown her cardboard dolls out on to the grass and moved in themselves?!

Feeling excitement thrumming in her chest, Katie shuffled closer and listened hard. The fairies seemed to be arguing.

"But we haven't even been given a *task*!" stormed the one with the dazzlingly blue hair.

"It's just so *unfair*!" And she stamped her foot to prove it.

Another shook her long fiery-orange locks and cried, "Maybe we don't *deserve* a task, after the way we behaved. Maybe we've been banished from Fairyland for ever!"

The blonde fairy twirled her plaits round and round anxiously. Katie noticed that, instead of bobbles, they were tied up with tiny daisies. "Oh, no, that can't be true!" she said gently. "I'm sure we'll be given a chance to prove we're sorry. She wouldn't just send us away for ever and ever . . . would she?"

They all fell silent then, looking horrified at the thought. They turned to the slim, fragile fairy with the jet-black hair, but she stayed silent, looking down and scuffing the sole of her tiny turquoise shoe

against the plastic floor.

The other three burst into life again, all shouting at once. Katie coughed loudly, but not one single fairy turned in her direction.

"Hello!" she called. But still nothing.

Katie decided that if she didn't do something drastic, she'd never get their attention. She leant forwards and put her hand over the kitchen window, plunging the room into darkness. *That* certainly made them notice her!

There were cries of "Eeek!" and "Help!" and "What's happening?!"

Katie took her hand away to find four frightened fairy faces staring out at her. "Oh, sorry! I didn't mean to scare you!" she said.

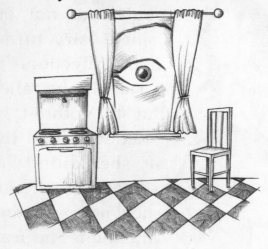

But the fairies stayed silent, staring. The flame-haired one was trembling and the one with the beautiful purple skirt gripped her friend's arm in fright. "Y-y-you can see us?" she stammered.

"That means she must believe in fairies!" gasped the blue-haired one, staring wide-eyed at her friends.

"I certainly do," said Katie, grinning. "Fairy stories are my favourite of all."

Katie suddenly remembered the manners Mum had taught her for meeting new people. "I'm Katie, pleased to meet you," she said, in her politest voice. She held out her hand for them to shake and then realized it wouldn't fit through the window, so she poked her little finger through instead. The fairies all leapt back in alarm. Then the one with the daisy plaits stepped forward and shook Katie's finger.

"I'm Daisy," she said, "and these are my friends – Bluebell, Rosehip and Snowdrop." She waved first towards the blue-haired fairy, then the bright orange-haired one and finally the jet-black-haired one, who gave Katie a nervous smile.

"This is amazing!" Katie exclaimed. "I didn't know you existed in real life."

"We don't actually live here on earth," Daisy explained. "Fairies only come to the human world to do tasks for the Fairy Queen."

"What kind of tasks?" asked Katie. She hadn't read about anything like this in her *Illustrated Treasury of Fairy Stories*.

"Things like helping flowers to grow and picking up litter," Rosehip told her. "The fairies come and do their tasks, and then they go home and get a reward."

"But *we're* not going home," wailed Bluebell. "We were sent here because we're always arguing and falling out. Fairies only go home when they've done their task, and we haven't even been *given* a task, so how can we *do* one? How can we go home? We'll be stuck here for ever and ever and we'll never see Fairyland again!"

That was when Snowdrop started sobbing quietly to herself. Daisy rushed over and put her arm round her. "Snowdrop, what's wrong?" she asked gently.

Snowdrop sniffled and clung tightly to Daisy. "Erm, it's just that, well, we *were* given a task," she mumbled.

Rosehip gasped and Bluebell stared. "What? When?" they demanded.

Daisy glared at them and they fell

25

silent. "Why didn't you tell us?" she asked Snowdrop gently.

"The Fairy Queen gave it to me just as we were leaving," Snowdrop sniffled. "You'd already gone sliding down into the sparkling whirlwind, to leave Fairyland, so you didn't see."

"Well, that's *good*, isn't it?" reasoned Bluebell. "We just have to do the task and then we can go home! Easy peasy!"

Snowdrop burst into fresh sobs. "But it's too *hard*," she wailed. "We'll never manage it. That's why I kept it a secret. It's the biggest task any fairy has ever been set, and I mean EVER! Look!" She rummaged in the purple petals of her skirt and thrust a piece of rolled up paper at Daisy, who unfurled it and read:

Fairy Task No. 45826

By Royal Command of the Fairy Queen

Terrible news has reached Fairyland. As you
know, the Magic Oak is the gateway between
Fairyland and the human world. The sparkling
whirlwind can only drop fairies off *here*.
Humans plan to knock down our special tree
and build a house on the land. If this happens,
fairies will no longer be able to come and help
people and the environment. You must stop
them from doing this terrible thing and make
sure that the tree is protected for the future.
Only then will you be allowed back into
Fairyland.

By order of Her Eternal Majesty
The Fairy Queen

PS You will need one each of the twelve
birthstones to work the magic that will save
the tree — but hurry, there's not much time!

The fairies all stared at each
other, stunned. For once there was
absolute silence.

"See what I mean?" said
Snowdrop, snuffling. She hung her

head and her shiny black hair fell forward over her tear-stained face.

"You're right – it's impossible!" cried Bluebell.

"And with no help at all, just this silly letter!" fumed Rosehip. The others gasped in shock and Rosehip's cheeks flushed red, clashing horribly with her hair. "Sorry, I didn't mean to criticize the Fairy Queen," she said quickly. She turned to the part of Katie she could see, which was precisely one eye and half a nose. "It's just, most fairies get some kind of instructions," she explained. "She hasn't even told us what birthstones *are*!"

Katie wished she could help, but she didn't know what birthstones were either.

Bluebell stamped her foot again, making all the little chairs round the

kitchen table shake. "I bet she *wants* us to fail, so she never has to see us again!"

"Now, now," said Daisy calmly. "You know that's not true, Bluebell. She's trusted us with the most important fairy task in the whole history of fairy tasks! We *have* to succeed. If we don't, the gateway between our worlds will be lost for ever – that spells the end of fairies helping humans!"

"Couldn't you use your fairy magic?" Katie asked, her huge voice booming round the tiny kitchen, making her feel like the giant in *Jack and the Beanstalk*. "Surely you can make anything happen just by wishing it? Can't you simply magic all the birthstones here? Or better still, just wish for the tree to be saved?"

The fairies all smiled at her sadly. "That's the problem with fairy stories written by humans," said Rosehip. "They all make us out to be superheroes. But we haven't got unlimited powers." She gestured to the kitchen table and Katie craned her neck to see the small bottle of sparkling dust sitting there. "We do have this fairy dust from the magic fountain in Fairyland, but we can only use it for small spells."

"Oh," said Katie. For once she

didn't have any more good ideas.

"Even if we find out what birthstones are—" Bluebell began.

". . .and collect them all—" Rosehip added.

". . .we still don't know how to do the magic," Snowdrop finished.

With that the fairies all sank into a gloomy mood, wings drooping.

"I'd like to help," said Katie, "but it's difficult when I'm so big. I've got a tree root sticking into my ribs and a horrible crick in my neck."

Bluebell's eyes shone. "That's something we *can* fix," she said. She picked up the bottle of fairy dust and skipped from the room.

The next moment the purple front door swung open and out she came. She unscrewed the cap and tipped up the bottle.

"Careful," warned Daisy from

the window, "don't use too much, that's all we've got."

"I know, don't fuss!" called Bluebell crossly. Katie watched as Bluebell carefully shook out a little of the sparkling dust on to the tiny blue door handle. What on earth was she planning to do?

"Right, you can shrink now," she told Katie triumphantly.

"What?!" Katie cried.

Bluebell grinned. "It's easy. All you have to it put your little finger on the doorknob and say, 'I believe in fairies' three times. Then

you'll shrink. That way you can be the same size as us and come into the house and help us work out what to do and. . ."

But Katie had stopped listening. What if something went wrong and she couldn't turn big again? What if she turned small but her clothes stayed big? Worst of all, what if she kept getting smaller and smaller and smaller until she was only a dot then a speck and then nothing at all? "I'm not sure," she mumbled.

Bluebell shrugged. "It's up to you."

All Katie's worries clanged away in her head. But then, she really, *really* wanted to go inside the dolls' house. She took a deep breath, squeezed her eyes shut and put her little finger on the tiny doorknob. The other three fairies leaned out of the kitchen window to watch.

"I believe in fairies," Katie whispered. "I believe in fairies. I believe in fairies."

Chapter 3

The first thing Katie felt was a strange tingling at the top of her head, like someone had sprinkled Sherbet Fizzwizz powder on it. Then there was a huge whooshing sound and suddenly everything around her was getting bigger and bigger and bigger. Except that it wasn't, of course. Actually, *she* was getting smaller and smaller and smaller. When she finally stopped shrinking she was the same size as Bluebell.

She looked around her at the dandelions, which now seemed as big as beach umbrellas. She smiled at Bluebell in amazement, and Bluebell grinned back. Then a low, sleepy buzzing filled the air. Katie whirled round to find a huge bumblebee coming straight towards her. "Argh!!!!!" she squealed, racing into the dolls' house and slamming the door shut.

The other fairies tumbled into the hall to greet her, giggling. "The bees won't hurt you," Daisy said. "Animals and insects love fairies."

"Yes, well, I'm *not* a fairy, am I?"

cried Katie. "And I'd rather not find out whether the bees can tell the difference!"

"I don't blame you!" said Rosehip.

Katie looked at Daisy's shimmering wings and bent her arm behind her, trying to feel whether or not she had any of her own. She was disappointed to find that she didn't.

"Sorry," said Snowdrop, "no wings. As you said, you haven't become a fairy."

"I wish I *could* be one!" said Katie fervently. But then she realized that if she were a real fairy she'd have to go back to Fairyland with the others when they'd finished the task and that she wouldn't get to live with Mum – in fact, Mum wouldn't even be able to *see* her! She decided that shrinking and turning big again was the best thing after all.

Katie was startled out of her thoughts by Bluebell dashing inside and grabbing her hand. "Come on," she cried, "I want to show you what I've done to my room."

"It's not *your* room!" said Rosehip. "We haven't decided on the rooms yet. Just because you've put up those horrid spotty curtains doesn't mean—"

"Yes, it does!"

"Does not!"

Daisy gave Katie a smile of sympathy as she was dragged upstairs by Rosehip *and* Bluebell.

As the three girls tumbled into the bedroom, Katie was amazed by what she saw. Bluebell had woven grass stems together to make a beautiful green patterned rug and painted bluebells on the wardrobe doors. She'd sewn two squares of

material together and stuffed them with moss, to make a cosy duvet. There were a few smaller rectangles of material laid carefully out on the bed, along with some dandelion petals, ready to be made into pillows. Flower stems were sticking out from under a chest of drawers, and when Katie tipped it up she discovered that it was very heavy – Bluebell had filled the drawers with stones! "I'm pressing some forget-me-nots, to make pictures," Bluebell explained, "for *my* walls."

"Lovely," said Katie, but Rosehip just stood with her hands on her hips and tossed her bright hair, eyes blazing. "They're not *your* walls! You know I want this room! I'm going to make a dragon-flower duvet and—"

"You can't!" shouted Bluebell. "I'm

making pillowcases with polka dots on, to match my curtains!"

"They're not *your* curtains!" Rosehip shouted back. Then suddenly they lunged at each other and fell back on to the bed, in a furious flurry of wings and petals. Rosehip had grabbed Bluebell's leg and Bluebell was pulling Rosehip's long flaming hair.

"Ow!"

"Youch!"

"Let go!"

"No, you first!"

"No, you!"

"Both of you stop that NOW!" Katie cried. The two fairies let go of each other and sat bolt upright, startled. Daisy and Snowdrop rushed into the room.

"Actually they're all *my* rooms," said Katie firmly. "And those curtains are made from *my* fabric! It's *my* dolls' house!"

All the fairies stared at her, shocked. "Sorry," muttered Bluebell. "We know it's your house really, because we saw you out here playing yesterday."

"That's why I felt like I was being watched!" said Katie. "It was you four!"

"Yes," said Daisy. "Then when

you left the dolls' house outside, we just thought, well hoped really, that maybe, um, that you'd forget all about it and we could stay here and—"

"We've got nowhere else to go!" wailed Snowdrop.

"If you won't let us stay, we'll have to camp out under a dock leaf!" said Rosehip, fuming, "and that is *no* fun in a thunderstorm, I can tell you!"

Katie smiled. "Calm down!" she said soothingly. "Of course you can stay here in the house, but no arguing, OK? You've got an important task to do!"

"OK," said Rosehip grudgingly. "I suppose Bluebell can have this room, seeing as she's already started decorating, but only if she helps me with the sewing on my

dragon-flower bedspread."

"Deal," said Bluebell, and they shook hands, though Katie thought their grip was a bit harder than necessary!

Snowdrop and Daisy were easy to sort out. Being a summer fairy, Daisy wanted the other sunny room looking out on to the almost-meadow, while winter sprite Snowdrop wanted the darker, cooler room facing the tree bark.

When everything was agreed, Snowdrop led Katie excitedly into her new room and climbed straight into the wardrobe, which she'd bewitched with fairy dust so that the doors really opened. "It's brilliant that you've got these big cupboards for playing hide and seek in," she said, smiling. "See!"

Katie couldn't help giggling.

"They're for your clothes!" she cried. "They're called wardrobes. Don't you have them in Fairyland?"

"But we're *wearing* our clothes," replied Snowdrop, looking confused.

The other fairies were all crowded in Snowdrop's doorway, listening.

"But when they get dirty you need to wash them and then when they're clean, you put them in the wardrobe," Katie explained.

"We only *have* these clothes," said Bluebell, twirling round to show off her blue ruffled skirt. "And anyway, fairies don't *get* dirty."

Katie grinned. "Lucky you! You won't be needing the bath either, then!"

"What's the bath?" asked Daisy.

"Do you mean that big potion-mixing pot in the little room?" ventured Rosehip.

"Yes!" spluttered Katie, shaking with laughter. "It sounds like you've never been in a human house! You could come home with me if you like, and see how wardrobes work, and baths, and I can show you *my* room—"

"Oh, no, we fairies never go inside humans' houses," shrieked Snowdrop, with a shudder. "There's no fresh air and we feel all cooped up and we can't breathe and it makes us go a bit . . . erm. . ."

"Crazy," finished Bluebell boldly.

"Besides, we need to stay here and get on with making some fairy lights," said Daisy anxiously. "We hardly slept a wink last night. Fairies are scared of the dark, you see."

Katie nodded. Now *that* was something they had in common. She still needed the night light on in the hall, even though she was almost seven and a half.

"I know how we can make some lights," said Rosehip. "All we need are some flowers, and a smidgeon of fairy dust!" She gave Daisy a wink and hurried down the stairs. Curious, they all followed her into the almost-meadow.

Once outside (and with Katie still on the lookout for buzzing bees!) they began picking daisies from the shorter grass by the garden fence. Katie could see Mum from there, sitting on the patio engrossed in a book about Matisse, the painter.

Katie felt glad she hadn't been missed. If she were suddenly called in, she'd have to hope that turning big again was just as quick as shrinking, so she could get back to the house before Mum came hunting for her.

To the fairies, the daisies were the size of sweeping brushes, and they could only hold a couple at a time. It was hard work, but soon they'd collected a big pile by the front door.

"Now we just need to take them inside the house and light them," said Rosehip. "But, oh, how will we hang them up?"

Katie smiled. "We could make them into a long daisy chain!" she suggested. "It's such fun, and then they'll be easy to put up!"

"Great idea!" said Bluebell

enthusiastically. "Erm, what's a daisy chain?"

So Katie showed the fairies how to thread the daisy stalks together.

"You're right, this *is* fun!" cried Rosehip, as the chain grew and grew. But after a while they got very wriggly and fidgety sitting on the grooves of the tree roots, so Bluebell gathered up some twigs and made a bench long enough for five. Katie held her breath as they all sat down, but the long strands of grass woven round the twigs held it firmly together. While they added more and more daisies to the chain, Rosehip taught Katie a fairy song, then Katie taught them the one about the kookaburra.

As they sang, Katie thought about how lonely she'd felt the day before, singing all by herself, and when they

finished, she couldn't help saying, "I really hope you'll be my friends."

Daisy grinned, dropped her part of the chain into her lap and gave Katie a big hug. "We hope you'll be ours, too!" she said merrily. Then all the fairies joined in the hug and some of the daisies got a bit squashed, but no one minded.

When the daisy chain was ready, Snowdrop went to fetch the bottle of fairy dust from the kitchen table. She shook some of the glittering powder into her hand and sprinkled it on to the daisy at the very end of the chain. It shrunk down to exactly the perfect size, and then the middle of each daisy began to glow softly, warm and welcoming and bright enough to chase away any shadows in the night. Katie squealed, amazed.

"It works!" cried Bluebell, and they all clapped and cheered and danced around in a big circle to celebrate.

Then they took the daisy chain inside and strung it all over the house, from room to room and in and out of the windows. "Just the kitchen to go now," said Katie.

"What's a kitchen?" asked Snowdrop.

Bluebell jumped up and down with her hand in the air, crying, "I know! I know! Is it that strange room with the big table in and all the empty drawers and cupboards? We've been trying to work out what it's for!"

"It's for making your food and eating it!" Katie laughed. "How can you not know that? Surely you must *eat*! Food keeps you alive . . . and it's delicious!"

"We fairies live on love and laughter," said Snowdrop. "We don't have food in Fairyland."

"Oh!" said Katie, smiling. "So your mouth must only be for talking! No wonder you have so many arguments!"

"Cheeky thing!" cried Rosehip, jostling her.

Katie beamed – this was just like

having real friends, friends that you could tease and be silly with and help when they had a problem.

Suddenly Katie caught a glimpse of her watch. "Oh no, I've to go! If I'm late in for lunch Mum'll come out looking for me and if she can't see me she'll worry and—"

"But what about the fairy task?" cried Bluebell. "We haven't even started working out—"

"I have to go now," Katie interrupted. "But I'll find out what these birthstone things are – promise." She looked at Daisy in panic. "But how do I. . ." she began.

"Don't worry," said Daisy gently, "just touch the

doorknob and say the spell again, then you'll turn big."

So Katie gave all the fairies a quick hug and hurried out of the door. Then she wrapped her fingers round the doorknob and whispered, "I believe in fairies. I believe in fairies. I believe in fairies."

This time it was her toes which fizzed and crackled, and then suddenly everything seemed to be getting smaller as she grew to her normal size. When she glanced down, the wooden bench Bluebell had made looked tiny. She could hardly believe that she'd actually been *sitting* on it!

"Bye!" she called, and four little fairy heads popped out of Bluebell's bedroom window to wave at her. Katie couldn't help smiling as she picked her way through the grasses

and wild flowers to the garden fence. "I've made some new friends," she whispered to herself. "And they're fairies! Who would ever believe it?!" For the first time since the move, she felt truly happy.

But as she dashed across the garden and hurried in for lunch, she had no idea that disaster was about to strike.

Of course, Mum didn't mean to spoil everything. As she dished out the macaroni cheese and tried to pile salad on to Katie's plate, she simply said, "Oh, darling, we both forgot about bringing your dolls' house inside last night. Could you be sure to remember it today? It would be such a shame if it got ruined."

Katie froze, her forkful of pasta hovering halfway to her mouth. She

hadn't even *thought* of that – that Mum might want her to bring the dolls' house inside. But how could she? Not now that she'd given the fairies a room each and said they could stay, and after they'd become her new friends and everything. "But I can't," she blurted out.

Mum raised her eyebrows. "Why ever not?" she asked, a little snappily. "I know that dolls' house wasn't the exact one you wanted, but I thought you'd care for it a bit better than this! I'm not made of money, Katie."

Katie's stomach lurched and she pushed her salad round and round her plate. She suddenly didn't feel hungry any more. She hated that Mum was upset about her leaving the dolls' house outside. Maybe if she explained, told the truth – well,

there was a tiny chance Mum might believe her. She took a deep breath. "I can't bring the dolls' house in because there are fairies living in it. . ." she began.

But Mum just frowned. "That's fun for a game, darling, but I'm being serious now," she said, crossly. "I want that dolls' house brought in."

Katie bowed her head, blinking back tears. They ate the rest of their lunch in silence.

Afterwards Katie went straight upstairs and read on her own until tea time. She felt so upset she hardly even bothered looking at the pictures and she turned the pages so hard that one ripped. Her mind whirled with questions – where would the poor fairies go? How would she tell them? Would they be angry, or even break friends with her? Katie wondered whether they'd still let her do the task with them. Even if she did find out what birthstones were, would they still *want* her help? They might not, not after she'd let them down so terribly. Oh, it was all such a mess!

At tea time, she had her tuna sandwich on her lap, watching TV,

trying not to think about the dolls'
house. It was all Mum's fault! Oh,
why wouldn't she just believe her?

But Katie couldn't be angry with
Mum. After all, she didn't know the
truth about the dolls' house, so she
didn't know what she was asking.
And besides, Katie hated it when
they fell out. So, when Mum came
up to kiss her goodnight, Katie gave
her a big hug and tried to look
happy.

"Have you brought it in yet?"
Mum asked.

"Oh, I'm sorry, I forgot again,"
said Katie, though it wasn't quite
true. "And now I'm ready for bed."

Mum sighed. "I'll have to go and
get it then," she muttered.

Katie grasped her arm, panic in
her eyes. "Oh no, please don't," she
begged. "I'll bring it in tomorrow

morning, first thing, before school –
I promise."

"OK, then," said Mum, giving her
a puzzled look. "But make sure you
do, or there'll be trouble!"

Once Mum had gone downstairs,
Katie got up again and looked out
of the window. She could just about
see over to the oak tree. The daisy
lights glowed dimly in the dolls'
house beneath it. The fairies must be

wondering why she hadn't come back out. She'd delayed the awful moment for as long as possible, but deep down she knew that there was no choice – if *she* didn't bring the dolls' house in, *Mum* would.

Either way, she was about to lose her new friends for ever.

Chapter 4

Katie lingered over her cornflakes the next day, as Mum washed up at the sink.

"I'm sorry you're still sulking, sweet pea," said Mum wearily. "But I meant what I said. If you don't go and get that dolls' house in before school, I'll do it myself."

"I'll go right now," said Katie, leaving her cereal bowl half full. She pulled on her school shoes and swished across the dewy lawn. Her

legs were weighed down, as though she were trying to walk in Rollerblades, and her heart felt just as heavy. She slipped through the fence, reached the oak tree and crouched down to peer into the dolls' house.

Bluebell and Rosehip were having a polka-dot pillow fight on Bluebell's bed, giggling and squealing. Daisy was flying around adjusting the fairy lights they'd made together.

Pink and purple flowers now spilled from window boxes made of woven grass. Just then, Snowdrop leaned out of the living room window, holding a tiny watering can made from an acorn cup, and began watering one of them.

"Hi, Katie," she called, breathless with excitement. "Do you like my flowers?" Katie nodded miserably, but Snowdrop didn't realize that anything was wrong and carried on chatting away. "You should have come back yesterday – we missed you so much! Daisy's going to paint her room today so she wants to know which shade of yellow you like best, and Rosehip's got another fairy song to teach you, and Bluebell's made up this brilliant game but we need five to play it, and—"

Katie sighed heavily. "I can't," she

mumbled. "I've got school, and I've also got some very bad news."

Soon, a shrunk-down Katie was standing in the kitchen of the dolls' house, with the four fairies gathered around her, all looking as utterly miserable as she did.

"I'm so sorry," she said again, "but I've got no choice. Mum insisted on me bringing the dolls' house in. I did try to explain about you, but she just wouldn't believe me. I'm so, so very sorry."

"It's OK," mumbled Daisy, trying to smile. "It's not your fault."

"Yes it is!" cried Bluebell suddenly, making Snowdrop jump.

"That's right!" added Rosehip, screwing her tiny fists up in anger. "*You* promised we could stay here! A promise is a promise and

I'm not leaving, so there!"

"But. . ." began Katie.

"Nor am I!" cried Bluebell. "You can't make us!"

"No, you can't make us!" echoed Snowdrop, startling everyone. Looking determined, she grabbed hold of the kitchen table and clung on. Bluebell and Rosehip liked this idea and leapt across the room to attach themselves to the kitchen cupboards with the tie-backs Bluebell had made for her polka-dot curtains.

"Look, I'm as upset as you are," said Katie, indignantly. "But it's *my* dolls' house and if I ask you to go you should go!" She glanced at Daisy for help but she just mumbled, "I'm not leaving all by myself," and clutched at a chair, avoiding Katie's glare.

"This is ridiculous!" Katie cried. "I have got school in half an hour and I need to bring the dolls' house inside, so please get out now!"

But the fairies just clung on tighter. Rosehip started a chant of, *No, no, we will not go!* and the others soon joined in. Then Bluebell stuck her tongue out at Katie, which was the final straw.

Katie lunged at her and pulled the blue polka-dot curtain tie-back from her wrist. But Bluebell just grabbed the cupboard handle instead and held on tight, kicking and squealing. Katie managed to pull Snowdrop off the table, but when she loosened her grip to make a grab for Daisy, Snowdrop wriggled away and wrapped herself tightly round a table leg like a koala. Katie started untying Rosehip then, but Bluebell leaned across and pinched her ribs until she had to let go. The four little

fairies were a lot stronger than they looked! Katie realized that there was only one way to deal with them. She got up from the floor and dusted herself down. "Fine!" she shouted. "You lot stay where you are, then! But the dolls' house is coming inside!"

And with that she marched out of the door, grabbed the doorknob and said the magic words. Soon she was her normal size and easily able to pick up the whole dolls' house – fairies or no fairies. With her other hand she snatched up her pencil case and bag of material, then marched back towards the house.

"No, Katie, please!" Daisy called through the kitchen window. "You know fairies don't like going inside human houses."

"Tough luck," said Katie, fuming. "You wouldn't get out so now you're going in!"

"But being in your house will make us go very, very—" began Rosehip, but Katie wasn't listening.

Once indoors she set the dolls' house down on the table.

"Are you coming?" she called up to Mum.

"OK, just putting some make-up on," came the reply from the bathroom.

Katie suddenly remembered Mum's meeting with Dorset Arts, about showing some of her paintings in their gallery. She didn't usually bother with make-up so Katie knew it must be important.

She peered into the dolls' house. Snowdrop was still clinging determinedly to the table leg but

Rosehip and Bluebell had run upstairs and hidden under Bluebell's bedspread. Daisy was leaning out of the living room window, setting a skewed flower box straight. "Please, Daisy, just come out," Katie begged, one last time.

But it wasn't Daisy who answered. It was Bluebell. She threw off the duvet and stood up on the bed, hands on hips. "Fine, we will," she called, pouting.

But if Katie had known what was about to happen, she'd have begged them to stay inside the dolls' house after all!

Bluebell stepped out of the front door on to a pile of magazines, then screeched and shot into the air as they slid on to the floor with a great *whumph*!

Rosehip tiptoed out and looked around. "So this is what it's like to be indoors," she gasped.

Daisy and Snowdrop followed after her, staring in wonderment.

"See, it's not so bad," said Katie, crouching down to gather up the magazines. "Maybe you could live in the dolls' house inside my house and. . ."

But suddenly all the fairies started panting and fidgeting and

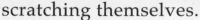

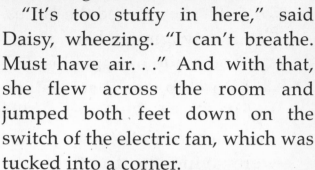

scratching themselves.

"It's too stuffy in here," said Daisy, wheezing. "I can't breathe. Must have air. . ." And with that, she flew across the room and jumped both feet down on the switch of the electric fan, which was tucked into a corner.

The fan started up, its head whizzing one way and then the other. Katie gasped as it caught on a pile of papers on the window sill and sent them flying into the air, then blew them all around the room. She dropped the magazines and leapt about, trying to grab them. She glanced nervously at the stairs, but Mum had the hairdryer going, so at least she couldn't hear the kerfuffle. Katie hoped that there was time to tidy everything up before she came down.

"Help me sort this mess out!" she ordered the fairies, but they ignored her.

"You made us come inside," said Rosehip, "so it serves you right!" She flew down to the floor, where Katie's toy ponies were lying in front of the television, and mounted an orange one.

"Catch," called Snowdrop, pulling the bottle of fairy dust from her pocket and throwing it to Rosehip. In one move Rosehip had plucked the bottle out of the air, wrenched out the cork and sprinkled fairy dust on to the plastic pony. It suddenly leapt into life and galloped up an armchair and on to the table, through Mum's paints and across her latest picture, leaving

little
coloured hoof
prints all over it.

"Stop!" cried Katie, but Rosehip just urged the pony on, round and round the canvas, ruining the painting.

"That looks like fun!" cried Snowdrop, diving down to the abandoned fairy dust bottle and bringing a white unicorn to life for herself. "Yee-hah!" she shouted, jumping aboard and galloping up the arm of the sofa. The unicorn's horn knocked off a mug that was balanced there. As it smashed on the wooden floor, cold coffee oozed over a pile of magazines and papers.

"Stop it!" Katie cried, but no one even heard her.

That was because Bluebell was jumping on the volume button of the TV remote control so that the voices and music got louder and louder and louder.

Katie stared in horror at the chaos around her. How could they do this to her? They were supposed to be her friends! She just couldn't stand it! She clamped her hands over her ears and screamed her loudest, most shriekingly ear-splitting scream.

That's when Mum dashed in. She grabbed the remote control and snapped off the TV, but she didn't seem to see Bluebell tumbling through the air. The ponies, just toys again, thudded to the floor.

Katie took her hands away from her ears and gaped at her mother. The room was a disaster zone. How could she even *begin* to explain? The only thing she could try was telling the truth. "It was the fairies, Mum," she blurted out. "Please, you've got to believe me. It really was! I tried to get them out of the dolls' house, to bring it in like you said, but—"

"How dare you be so cheeky!" shouted Mum, stopping Katie dead. "My painting's ruined! I was taking it with me to the meeting. It's my

best work! How could you do all this, just because I asked you to bring that dolls' house in?"

Mum stared at Katie, waiting for an answer, but she felt so awful she couldn't say anything at all.

"I'm very disappointed in you, Katie," Mum continued. "Now clear it all up, this instant!" And with that she stormed back upstairs, slamming the living room door behind her.

Katie stood stunned, her knees trembling and her stomach flipping over and over. She'd rarely seen Mum so angry. She collapsed on to the sofa and started to sob and sob.

Chapter 5

The next moment, Katie felt four little fairies land in her lap. She blinked at them through her tears but they wouldn't meet her eye, they were all hanging their heads in shame.

"Katie, we're so sorry," said Daisy eventually. "I don't know what got into us. We didn't mean to cause such trouble – we were just so angry and upset about losing our new home and friend, and we hate being in human houses!"

"I noticed!" Katie sniffled.

"We'll go now," said Bluebell sadly. "We've caused enough trouble."

"We really are sorry," said Rosehip.

"Yes, we really are," echoed Snowdrop.

And with that all the fairies took to the air and flew towards the open back door.

Katie suddenly sat upright. "Wait," she called, "I think I've had an idea. If we can make the house even tidier than it was before, it would show Mum how sorry I am. And if I can make her understand how much I want to keep the dolls' house outside, there's a tiny chance she'll let me. But we'll have to be quick – I leave for school soon.

80

And it means being inside for a bit longer."

"We can manage another few minutes," said Bluebell, taking some deep breaths.

"We should just be able to do it before your mum comes back down – with a little sprinkle of fairy dust to help us," added Snowdrop.

"Then let's go!" cried Katie, leaping to her feet. And with that they all started whirling round the room, cleaning and tidying. Daisy turned off the fan, Rosehip and Bluebell got a sponge from the kitchen sink and flew back and forth over the coffee spill, soaking it

up. Katie collected up the papers and placed them firmly under a big beach pebble, then scooped the magazines back on to the table, and Snowdrop fixed the painting, dabbing fairy dust on each tiny painted hoof print so it vanished.

Then, in the kitchen, Daisy and Snowdrop helped Katie to put her packed lunch together while Rosehip and Bluebell painted a sorry-card with Mum's paints.

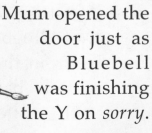

Mum opened the door just as Bluebell was finishing the Y on *sorry*.

Bluebell squeaked and quickly dropped the paintbrush back into its pot so that Mum wouldn't see it hovering in mid-air!

When Katie came through from the kitchen, lunch box in hand, Rosehip tugged at her arm and pointed to the card. Katie smiled, picked it up and held it out to Mum. "I'm so sorry I made such a mess," she said.

Mum sighed deeply and took the card. "What am I going to do with you?" she muttered. Then she pulled Katie into a big hug and added, "I shouldn't have been so hard on you. I'm just a bit stressed out this morning – this gallery meeting is so important."

"I know – I'm so sorry. But I fixed your painting."

"Wow!" cried Mum. "how did you do that?"

But Katie decided it was best not to answer. Instead she took a deep breath and twisted her ring round and r o u n d nervously on her finger. "Mum," she said carefully, "well, you know how important the gallery meeting is to you? It's just ... if something was that important to *me*, would you think about allowing it?"

Mum smiled. "Well, I'd have to know what the thing was first," she said gently.

"I'd like to keep the dolls' house under the oak tree," Katie barely whispered, hardly daring to hope. "You see, I'm making it into a home for the fairies and fairies can't live indoors."

Before Mum could say no, Katie led her over to the dolls' house and clicked the catch open so that it folded out like a book. Then she showed her everything they'd done inside – pretending it was all her own work, of course! "Look, I've already made little bedspreads and curtains and rugs for them," she explained, "and window boxes with flowers and. . ."

"Gosh, they're beautiful!" Mum gasped. "What a gorgeous shade of purple."

"I'm even painting this room yellow," Katie continued, pointing into Daisy's bedroom. "I've mixed a few different shades, and I'm going to decide which is the nicest." Daisy was hovering by the back door and Katie caught her eye. The little fairy

waved her crossed fingers in the air hopefully.

Mum looked at everything very carefully, even though they were getting late for school. "Wow, Katie, you really have done a wonderful job of making this your very own," she said. "I'm so sorry darling, I got it all wrong. I thought you'd left the dolls' house outside because you didn't care about it, but I can see now that you really do."

"So can it go back under the oak tree?" asked Katie. She held her breath and watched the fairies hovering, fingers crossed, eyes squeezed shut.

"Yes," said Mum. "In fact, let's go and put it there right now."

Katie grinned and gave Mum a big hug, murmuring "Thank you,

thank you, thank you," into her ear. Then she clipped the dolls' house shut and together they took it back out to the tree, the fairies following along at Katie's shoulder, twirling and dancing in the air.

Katie placed the dolls' house carefully on the ground and the gleeful fairies touched down on to the roof. "See you after school," she whispered to them.

"Who are you talking to?" asked Mum.

Katie started. "Oh, erm, just the fairies," she said.

"That's such a lovely game, darling," said Mum, taking Katie's hand. "What a wonderful imagination you've got. And what are the names of these fairies, then?"

And so, as they headed back to the house, Katie told Mum all about Bluebell, Rosehip, Snowdrop and Daisy, knowing that she wouldn't believe a single word!

Chapter 6

Katie tugged at Mum's hand all the way back from school, almost making her run down the street! She'd looked up birthstones in the library during their quiet reading time and made a list of them – and she'd found, to her amazement, that she already had one! As soon as they got home she threw down her satchel and ran out to the dolls' house. Once there, she checked that Mum wasn't looking, but she

needn't have worried – the gallery meeting had been a great success and Mum was busy indoors doing some rough sketches for new paintings.

Katie put her little finger on the tiny blue doorknob and closed her eyes. "I believe in fairies, I believe in fairies, I believe in fairies," she whispered. With a fizzing at the top of her head and the peculiar feeling that everything around her was getting bigger, she shrunk down to fairy size.

The fairies came dashing out of the dolls' house to meet her and they all had a big hug. Katie felt happiness welling up inside her – it was just so wonderful that everything was back to normal and they were all friends again!

"I've got a—" she began, but

Daisy was tugging at her hand and jiggling about with excitement. "Come and pick a yellow for my room!" she gabbled. "I've been waiting for you all day! These girls are hopeless – we can't agree on which shade and anyway, Bluebell keeps saying it should be blue!"

"Bluebell thinks *everything* should be blue!" Rosehip laughed.

So they all tumbled inside and

together Katie and Daisy picked out the most cheerful sunshiny yellow of all. They set to work with her paints and brushes, which were like brooms in their tiny hands, and soon every wall was yellow! Then Katie went to help Bluebell put the finishing touches to her new room (which was all blue, of course!).

"Oh, we just need the curtain tie-backs," said Bluebell. She blushed a

deep pink and said, "They're still in the kitchen from when we, erm, well, when we tied ourselves to the cupboards."

Katie smiled. "I'll get them," she said, to show that there were no hard feelings. She went galloping down the stairs just as she did in her own house. As she picked up the tie-backs from the kitchen table, the sunlight slanting in through the window caught on her ring, lighting it up with a red flash. She suddenly remembered the exciting news she had to tell her friends.

She raced back upstairs and went crashing into Daisy's room. "I found out what birthstones are!" she cried breathlessly, as all the fairies gathered round in excitement. "They're different gems, and each one is linked to a month of the year.

I've made a list of them." She rummaged in her pocket and pulled out the piece of paper she'd noted them down on, and they all read it. "There's diamond and pearl and opal and topaz and so many more!" squealed Snowdrop.

"Now we know what to look for we can make a start on the fairy task!" cried Daisy.

Katie beamed. "Better still, I've got one already!" She giggled, waggling her hand in the air. The fairies all peered at the ring that Auntie Jane had given her. "It's garnet," she told them, "the January birthstone. My

birthday's not in January, but Auntie Jane's is. She gave this to me because it got too small for her when she grew up!"

The fairies all jumped up and down, squealing with excitement.

"See, the Fairy Queen wants you to succeed, just like Daisy said," reasoned Katie. "She must have known I had the right gemstone! Maybe she sort of made me forget the dolls' house that first night, so that we'd meet and I'd give you the first birthstone!"

"So she does care after all!" cried Snowdrop.

"Maybe we really *can* do this task," said Rosehip.

"But, Katie, will you help us?" asked Daisy.

"Of course – you're my friends," said Katie. "We must all save the

tree together. The person planning to knock it down must be a builder of some kind – I'm sure I can find out who it is, and what he's up to. Then we'll know how long we've got to make the magic work." Katie twisted the garnet ring back on to her finger. "And I'll take extra care of this from now on."

"Now we just have to find all the other birthstones," said Snowdrop, frowning.

"Let's leave that until tomorrow," said Katie. "We've made a good start, and besides, it's almost time for me to go, and I still haven't seen what you've done to the rest of the house!"

So the fairies gave Katie a grand tour and showed her all their efforts. Bluebell's beautiful pressed-flower pictures adorned the walls

and Snowdrop's window boxes had sprung twice as many blooms under her loving care. The living room had been transformed with rose-petal covers on the sofas, and Rosehip had shaken a dash of fairy dust on to the plastic piano so that it really worked.

"You've made the dolls' house really perfect," Katie exclaimed. "But it just needs one more thing."

She headed upstairs, smiling a mysterious smile, and returned with one of the paintbrushes from Daisy's room. They all followed her outside, curious, and watched as she painted

The Fairy House

on the front door in beautiful curly lettering. Then she turned to the fairies and smiled. "It's not the

dolls' house any more – it's the Fairy House now," she declared. "I'm giving it to you. Welcome to your new home!"

"Oh, wow!" they all cried, swamping her in hugs. "Thank you, thank you, thank you!"

Beaming, Katie hugged her new friends back, as hard as she could. "Will you play the piano for us, Rosehip?" she asked, when they finally broke apart.

"I'd love to!" cried Rosehip.

Soon, beautiful tinkling music filled the Fairy House and they all joined in the fairy song, dancing and singing and whirling and spinning and laughing, just like real friends do.

The End

Bluebell
Spring fairy

Likes:

blue, blue, blue and more blue,
turning somersaults in the air, dancing

Dislikes:

coming second, being told what to do

Daisy
Summer fairy

Likes:

everyone to be friends, bright sunshine,
cheery yellow colours, smiling

Dislikes:

arguments, cold dark places,
orange nylon dresses

Rosehip
Autumn fairy

Likes:

riding magic ponies, telling Bluebell
what to do, playing the piano, singing

Dislikes:

keeping quiet, boring colours,
not being the centre of attention!

Snowdrop
Winter fairy

Likes:

singing fairy songs, cool quiet places, riding her
favourite magical unicorn, making snowfairies

Dislikes:

being too hot, keeping secrets

Don't miss the rest of the series!

The Fairy House

Fairies to the Rescue

Daisy
x

Kelly McKain